Gullibility Factor

by Peter Yates

Gullibility Factor
by Peter Yates

©COPYRIGHT 2008 Peter Yates

First Published 2009 by Random Cactus
ISBN 978-0-9559924-1-4

Rights of Performance are controlled by:

Random Cactus

New Place, Romeland Hill, St. Albans,

Herts. AL3 4ET

Phone: 01727 838540

Fax: 01727 843540

Email: random_cactus@yahoo.co.uk

Web: www.randomcactus.co.uk

from whom a license for performance should be obtained.

It is an infringement of the Copyright to give any performance or public reading of the play before the license has been issued.

Gullibility Factor

was first performed at Augustine's at the Edinburgh Fringe, August 2008, with the following cast:

Mariele Runacre Temple Suzanne, Jessica, Alice, Eva.
Reuben Anderson Lobb, Scenic, Bob, Ryan.
Jack Bowman Clubber, Mack, Dave, Ted, Morris.
Ceri Gifford Girlfriend, Alex, Carol, Cal.

Lighting & Sound by Alex Campbell
Stage Manger – Florence Goodwin
Directed by Jenny Runacre

Produced by Peter Yates & Mariele Runacre Temple
for Random Cactus & The Wireless Theatre Company

The show can be downloaded from:
www.wirelesstheatrecompany.co.uk

1. Encounters With Doormen
part 1

2. Canada Dry

3. They Never Say Fuck on the Archers

4. Chance Meeting

5. Corkage

6. First Casualty

7. Encounters With Doormen
epilogue

Encounters With Doormen

part 1

Encounters With Doormen
by   Peter Yates
©COPYRIGHT 2008 Peter Yates

First Published 2009 by Random Cactus
ISBN 978-0-9559924-1-4

Rights of Performance are controlled by:
Random Cactus
New Place, Romeland Hill, St. Albans,
Herts. AL3 4ET
Phone: 01727 838540
Fax: 01727 843540
Email: random_cactus@yahoo.co.uk
Web: www.randomcactus.co.uk

from whom a license for performance should be obtained.

It is an infringement of the Copyright to give any performance or public reading of the play before the license has been issued.

Characters:

Lobb

Clubber

Girl

Manager

Outside a Club. Tonight.

Part One.

> *Lobb is standing in front of Club entrance. Clubber and Girlfriend enter.*

CLUBBER: Er… excuse me. How much is it to come in?

LOBB: Ten quid, sir. Each.

CLUBBER: OK. Bit on the steep side.

LOBB: Steep, sir?

CLUBBER: Well…

LOBB: So you don't wish to come in, sir. You can't afford it? Or you're a bit of a cheap-skate?

GIRLFRIEND: [*giggles*]

CLUBBER: I see. They have comedians on the outside now, as well.

GIRL: [*giggles*]

CLUBBER: Anymore? Or is that the full repertoire?

GIRL: [giggles]

CLUBBER: Where do we pay?

LOBB: Inside, sir.

CLUBBER: OK. Thanks, Razor. Come on, Bella.

LOBB: I'm called Nutter, sir. Not Razor.

CLUBBER: Really? I meant as in razor-sharp wit.

GIRL: Why Nutter?

LOBB: Because I'm a Nutter.

CLUBBER: Right. I see. Come on, let's go in. Enough of this idle chit-chat.

LOBB: You can't go in, sir.

CLUBBER: Sorry?

LOBB: You can't go in, sir.

CLUBBER: Why not?

LOBB: Because I say so.

GIRL: You say so?

LOBB: That's what I said.

CLUBBER: Why can't we go in?

LOBB: I didn't say she couldn't go in. Just you, sir.

CLUBBER: Well, we're together. Obviously. She's not going to go in without me, now, is she?

LOBB: I don't know, sir.

GIRL: I'm not going in alone. We're together.

LOBB: I'm pleased for you. So you're both not going in. Have a good night, sir. Madam.

GIRL: But why can't he go in - and don't say I said so?

CLUBBER: There's got to be a reason.

LOBB: Jeans, sir.

CLUBBER: What? I'm not wearing jeans.

LOBB: Exactly. No-one's allowed in without jeans. Club rules.

GIRL: So it's changed since last week has it?

CLUBBER: No, you're not getting me on that one, sunshine. Club rules – ha!

LOBB: Trainers.

CLUBBER: Oh, so trainers are banned, are they?

LOBB: That's right.

GIRL: New Rule, is it?

LOBB: Yep. Came in today.

CLUBBER: [*removing shoes*] That's fine then. No trainers. I'll check them at the door.

GIRL: We all dance without shoes in there. So, can we go in now?

LOBB: I'm afraid not, sir.

GIRL: Why not?

CLUBBER: Come on. Lay it on me. What lame excuse have you got now that we can check out with the management?

LOBB: It's your face sir.

CLUBBER: My face?

GIRL: What's wrong with his face?

LOBB: I don't like it. Sir.

CLUBBER: Oh, great. You don't like it. Suppose I don't like yours.

LOBB: Then you would be at liberty not to let me into your house. Sir.

GIRL: Look, you can't stop someone going in because of their face.

LOBB: I just have, madam.

GIRL: That's facial prejudice.

Pause.

LOBB: Are you calling me a facist?

GIRL: Yes. That's exactly what I'm calling you. A facist. And, funnily enough, it's almost spelt the same way as fascist. Now add that to your comedic repertoire.

CLUBBER: Now, you got told, Pal. So let us in or get the manager here.

***Lobb** punches girl in the mouth.*

CLUBBER: Hey! What the fuck...

GIRL Aaaahh! He it me. In the mouth! I'm bleeding!

CLUBBER: You hit her. I want the manager here. Now! You can't go round hitting people in the mouth.

LOBB: I just have, sir.

CLUBBER: Get the manager!

LOBB: No, sir.

CLUBBER: What? Right I'm calling the police. You can't go round hitting people. Hitting a woman in fact. You're gonna get sacked...

LOBB: I didn't hit her, sir.

CLUBBER: What...?

LOBB: I didn't hit her.

GIRL: Yes you did, you bastard. Look, my lip's bleeding.

CLUBBER: You hit her – punched her – in the mouth. You said you did!

LOBB: I don't think so, sir. I think you will find, sir, that she walked into my outstretched arm as I tried to prevent her from illegally entering the Cub.

CLUBBER: Oh, yes…?

LOBB: I was simply dong the job I am paid to do, sir.

CLUBBER: You're not going to get away with this. Look – CCTV…

LOBB: I think you will find, sir, that the CCTV pictures completely corrugate my version of the incident.

CLUBBER: Corrugate? Don't you mean "corroborate"? [*aside*] Thick cockney twat.

LOBB: That's what I said sir. Corrugate.

CLUBBER: D'you hear that, Bella? He's saying "corrugate" when he means "corroborate". The thick, cockney...

GIRL: Why are you analyzing his vocabulary? He punched me in the mouth! I'm bleeding! He may have dislodged a tooth.

CLUBBER: Oh, big word, corrugate. Do you want to come and mend my roof?

LOBB punches Clubber in the mouth.

CLUBBER: Aaaargh! He hit me. Did you see that? The wanker hit me. The compete fucking wanker hit me! In the mouth. The wanker! You're a wanker, mate, A complete wanker. You can't go round hitting people. In the mouth. Customers. I'm a customer, you know. You wanker. You're a wanker. A complete fucking wanker. You need help, mate. Therapy. Anger management. You're a fucking wanker mate, do you know hat? A fucking cockney twat wanker. Do you know what he is?

GIRL: Yeah, I get the picture. A wanker.

LOBB: Are you corroborating that madam.

GIRL: No. Not at all. Those are his own personal views. I'm sure you are a very gentle person who loves small children and animals [*aside*] to eat.

LOBB: Come now sir, let me help you up. A little tipsy, are we? Had a little too much to drink? I tell you what sir, I'll call you a taxi.

CLUBBER: Get off me! I don't want a fucking taxi! I'm having you for assault.

LOBB: Assault and buggery, sir? I do hope you are not questioning my sexual preferences, sir. Because I might get a little upset and angry about that?

CLUBBER: It's assault and battery, you thick…

CLUBBER/LOBB/GIRL: …cockney twat.

LOBB: Yes, sir. We get the picture. Don't we madam? And, madam - here's a handkerchief for your lip. There's a cab. Let me help you.

GIRL: Get off me! We're calling the police.

LOBB: I wouldn't advise that, madam.

GIRL: Of course you wouldn't because you'll be arrested.

LOBB: [holding up mobile camera 'phone] I doubt it. But what would happen, madam, sir, is this. Your picture would be circulated to every doorman at every club, pub and gig in the city and you would never gain entry again. Anywhere. Ever. Us doormen stick together. We watch out for each other. We're like a brotherhood. When we spot a troublemaker we make sure that they never cause trouble again. That is our code. Search and eject. That is our motto. So is sir gong to call the police?

[*all charm and syrup*] Or would sir and madam like to come in now?

GIRL: In...?

CLUBBER: Into the club? What are you talking about? You just wouldn't let us... you just hit us...! You're a nutter!

LOBB: Oh, thank you, sir. For using my nickname. I like to be called Nutter. It means we're all friends. Together. Funny, isn't it? I don't seem to mind your face anymore. In you go. Quick. Before I change my mind.

Lobb *ushers them and they scamper in, bewildered. Enter female* **Manager**.

MANAGER: What was that all about, Nutter?

LOBB: Not a lot. She suggested I was almost a fascist.

MAN: Bastards. What a fucking insult. Can't they get it into their thick heads that we are complete, dyed-in-the-wool fascists

	right down to the swastika tattoos on our...
LOBB:	...knuckles. Yeah. I think they got the message.
MAN:	Seeya, Nutter.
LOBB:	Yeah. Seeya, Adolf.

Manager exits. Lobb cracks his knuckles and speaks to audience.

LOBB: Funny. I always feel better once I've hit someone.

<u>Blackout.</u>

Canada Dry

Canada Dry
by Peter Yates
©COPYRIGHT 2008 Peter Yates

First Published 2009 by Random Cactus
ISBN 978-0-9559924-1-4

Rights of Performance are controlled by:

Random Cactus

New Place, Romeland Hill, St. Albans,

Herts. AL3 4ET

Phone: 01727 838540

Fax: 01727 843540

Email: random_cactus@yahoo.co.uk

Web: www.randomcactus.co.uk

from whom a license for performance should be obtained.

It is an infringement of the Copyright to give any performance or public reading of the play before the license has been issued.

Characters:

Mack, *male, early twenties.*

Alex, *female, early twenties.*

Scenic, *male, early twenties.*

Suzanne, *female, late twenties, North American accent.*

A PR Office.

An oblong table, set up for a meeting – water bottles, mixer bottles, glasses, pads etc. **Mack** *sits at one end,* **Alex** *at the other and* **Scenic** *at side [facing audience] with a spare chair next to him.*

The three are dressed for the business environment but don't look particularly smart. They are in mid-conversation, loud, animated, about football.

Enter **Suzanne**, *immaculately dressed, carrying lap-top. Immediate silence. She pauses momentarily then moves to the spare place, puts lap-top on table.*

SUZANNE: Hi. Don't stop on my account. Do go on. It sounded interesting.

Embarrassed coughs, eyes down, doodling on pads, pouring drinks etc.

SUZANNE: No, really. Do go on. Finish your conversation. What was it about?

MACK: Football.

SUZANNE: Oh, good.

ALEX: So. Is Fabian Capello the right man for the job? [*or similar topical question*]

SUZANNE: Erm… who…

ALEX: Ah.

SUZANNE: Sorry. I'm not well up on football.

MACK: Evidently.

SCENIC: So. End of conversation.

SUZANNE: Well, anyway. Let me introduce myself. I'm Suzanne…

MACK: You're an American.

SUZANNE: No I'm not, actually.

SCENIC: You've got an American accent.

SUZANNE: North American. I'm actually from...

SCENIC: North America...

SUZANNE: ...Canada.

SCENIC: I've been to America. Florida. Disneyland.

ALEX: Disney <u>World</u>, you loser. Disney <u>Land</u> is in California.

SCENIC: Whatever. Is it?

MACK: San Francisco.

SUZANNE: Los Angeles, actually.

SCENIC: I thought you weren't American.

SUZANNE: I'm not. But I do know where Disneyland ...

SCENIC: Disney <u>World</u>. I went to Disney <u>World</u>. In Florida.

SUZANNE: Fascinating. But we should get on. I'm Suzanne ...

MACK: Mack.

ALEX: Alex.

SCENIC: Scenic.

SUZANNE: Scenic. That's an interesting name. Nick name?

SCENIC: Scenic Route.

SUZANNE: I'm sorry?

ALEX: Scenic Route. Moot.

MACK: It's cockney rhyming slang.

SUZANNE: Is it?

SCENIC: Like Apples.

SUZANNE: What?

ALEX: Apples and Pears...

MACK: Stairs.

SUZANNE: Erm...

ALEX: Or boat

SUZANNE: Boat?

SCENIC: Face.

SUZANNE: Face?

MACK: Boat race. Face.

SUZANNE: I...

MACK: Or my favourite: Merchant.

SUZANNE: Merchant?

ALEX: Merchant banker.

MACK/SCENIC: Wanker.

They laugh. ***Suzanne*** *doesn't.*

SCENIC: Or <u>my</u> favourite…

ALEX: Tommy.

SUZANNE: Tommy?

MACK: Tommy Tucker…

SCENIC: Mother…

SUZANNE: Yes, I think I'm there, now. Thanks.

SCENIC: So I'm scenic.

ALEX: Scenic Route.

MACK: Moot. Because he says "moot" all the time. "That's a moot point".

SCENIC: Yes. I do. I say it all the time.

ALEX: He does. Moot. Moot point.

SUZANNE: Well good. Sense of humour. I appreciate a sense of humour.

MACK: Do you? I thought Americans didn't have a sense of humour.

SUZANNE: No. That's Irony. Americans don't have a sense of irony. And I'm not an American.

ALEX: She's not an American.

SCENIC: Isn't she? What is she, then?

ALEX: Canadian. Aren't you? From Canada.

SUZANNE: That's right. So I think we'd better cut to the chase, don't you?

MACK: That's an American expression.

SUZANNE: Your point?

MACK: I don't have one.

SCENIC: It's a moot point, then!

The Three laugh, uproariously, ott.

SUZANNE: Yeah. I get it. Very funny.

ALEX: <u>We</u> thought so.

SUZANNE: So. Down to business. Head office have sent me…

MACK: Head office… where exactly…

SUZANNE: You don't know where head office is…?

***Mack** gestures ignorance.*

SUZANNE: Head office is in Saskatoon.

MACK: In?

SUZANNE: Saskatchewan.

SCENIC/ALEX/MACK: [ott American accents] Saskatoon in Saskatchewan!

SUZANNE: Ah. So you did know.

SCENIC/ALEX/MACK: Saskatoon in Saskatchewan!

SCENIC: Say it again.

SUZANNE: Why?

SCENIC: Oh please, please…

MACK: Yes, please…

ALEX: Go on, please…

SUZANNE: Saskatoon in Saskatchewan.

ALEX: Brilliant. You say it really well.

SUZANNE: Thank you.

SCENIC: Yeah, it sounds good with an American accent.

SUZANNE: My accent...

MACK: So you've come all the way from China?

SUZANNE: What?

MACK: China. Saskatchewan is in China.

SUZANNE: No...

MACK: It's a province. I think.

SCENIC: And Saskatoon – well you can't get a more Chinese name than that.

SUZANNE: Believe me, Saskatchewan is in Canada.

SCENIC: You're having a giraffe. Down the Chinky I always have Sizzling Saskatchewan Chicken with bamboo shoots and Chinese mushrooms don't I?

ALEX: Yep, it's your favourite.

SUZANNE: I think you mean Szechwan Chicken with bamboo shoots and Chinese mushrooms. <u>Szechwan</u> is a province of China. <u>Saskatchewan</u> is a province of Canada. Believe me. I know. I live there.

ALEX: She ought to know.

MACK: She's an American. Believe her.

SUZANNE: I am NOT an American. I am a Canadian.

SCENIC: It's a moot point.

Silence, then suppressed laughter.

SUZANNE: Shall we move on. Or do you want to sit around and play silly buggers all day?

MACK/ALEX: Ooooh! [*the "get her" sound*]

SCENIC: No. No. She's right. Let's move on [*accent*]. If you've taken the trouble to fly all the way in from China.

ALEX: Ahem!

SCENIC: Oops! My bad. From [*exaggerated accent*] Saskatoon in Saskatchewan, Can-nay-dee-a. Then the least we can do is make you feel at home.

SUZANNE: Thank you.

MACK: Sorry that Donny, Greg and Celine couldn't be here today

SUZANNE: Who…?

SCENIC: Donny… You know Donny don't you? No? Donald? Donald Sutherland?

SUZANNE: For God's…

MACK: And Greg. Rudeszci. The Tennis Player.

SCENIC: Retired.

ALEX: Did you say retarded?

SCENIC: It's a moot point.

ALEX: And Celine of course. Celine Dion. Three very famous Canadians.

SCENIC: The only three famous Canadians

MACK: Though to be fair Greg is actually naturalised British now.

MACK: And retarded.

SCENIC: That's a moot point.

ALEX: He does still have an American accent.

SCENIC: That's a moot point.

ALEX: And what about Keiffer, eh?

MACK/ SCENIC: Who?

ALEX: Keiffer Sutherland. You know. *Twenty-Four*. Jack Bauer. The real-time show. Twenty-four hours in twenty-four episodes.

MACK: That's American. Fox Network.

ALEX: Donny's little boy. Keiffer.

SCENIC: He's American. He's definitely American.

ALEX: But his Daddy's Canadian.

MACK: He was born in London.

ALEX: Was he?

SUZANNE: Does it matter? Does it really matter? Is this what you do all day? Celebrity trivia? No wonder this department is going down the tubes. Does it matter?

SCENIC: It's a moot point.

SUZANNE: I think we've had enough of the quirky little catch phrase, too, don't you? I think we need to get our grown-up heads on, stop fucking about and get some serious discussion going. Like how are we going to stop the terminally declining downward fucking-spiral that this department seems to be locked into. OK?

Silence.

SCENIC: O-kaay.

ALEX: Well, I think that's a little on the harsh side…

MACK: Er… Ms …

SUZANNE: Call me Suzanne.

MACK: OK. Thank you. Ms. Suzanne… I'm not quite sure that some of your language is appropriate for a serious business environment.

SUZANNE: Oh, aren't you now. What specific language would you be talking about.

MACK: Well…er… spiral…

SUZANNE: Well, Mack, seeing as how you seem to like all things Chinese, an old Chinese proverb for you. If you don't like the fucking heat get out the fucking kitchen.

MACK: Fine. Fine. Point taken

SCENIC: It's a…

SUZANNE: Don't!

SCENIC: Sorry.

SUZANNE: Now. This department appears to have one principal function. You are responsible for marketing one, I believe, just one of this company's extensive range of cosmetic products. That particular product…

Scenic *puts his hand up.*

SUZANNE: Yes?

SCENIC: What's irony, Ms?

SUZANNE: Do I sound like an American?

SCENIC: Yes.

SUZANNE: Well I wouldn't know what irony is, would I? That's irony.

SCENIC: Oh.

SUZANNE: That particular product, erstwhile best seller, former market leader, used to be called "Dawn".

MACK: Right

ALEX: Yes.

SUZANNE: And you changed it.

MACK: As part of our marketing strategy going forward.

ALEX: Agreed.

SCENIC: Which everyone endorsed.

SUZANNE: OK. You changed it to the charmingly sounding exotic name – if I can pronounce it correctly in my twangy North American lilt – "Oital Lef".

SCENIC: Perfect!

MACK: Sounds great, doesn't it?

ALEX: Magical.

SCENIC: Hints of far eastern mystery.

ALEX: Exotic, swirling jasmine-scented mists…

SCENIC: …enticing beautiful young women…

ALEX: …with long flowing hair…

MACK: …and tight-fitting white underwear…

ALEX: …into a dreamy, romantic world…

SCENIC: ...where their wildest fantasy can be fulfilled.

ALEX: Brilliant copy-writing, I thought.

MACK: A wonderful marketing strategy.

SCENIC: "Oitel Lef"!

ALEX: It's Chinese for Sunrise.

MACK: That's right.

SCENIC: Inspired eh? Used to be "Dawn"; now "Oitel Lef" – Sunrise. In Chinese.

SUZANNE: Yeah. It also happens to spell "fellatio" backwards.

ALEX: Does it?

MACK: I never knew that.

ALEX: "Oital Lef"... er... [*writing*] er... yes it does. Stone me! Look.

MACK: So it does. Look Scenic.

SCENIC: Oh, yes! Well fancy that! [*hand up*] What does fellatio mean, Ms?

MACK: Cock suck.

SCENIC: [*hurt*] Hey, there's no need to be like that. Just 'cos I don't know. Tell him, Ms.

SUZANNE: He's right. At its crudest, which seems to be the lowest common denominator here, it means to suck a cock and I don't believe for a moment you didn't know that and I don't believe for a moment that you didn't know it spelt that backwards and I don't believe for a moment it was accidental.

SCENIC: Ah.

SUZANNE: It could, of course, have been an absolute masterstroke had it been handled properly. But it wasn't. It was inept. It was stupid. It was maladroit, heavy-handed, lacking in all sense and sensitivity and it's possibly illegal. Frankly, now that I've met the team behind the concept, the best word I can use is klutzy. And since its mass removal from supermarket shelves last week with no explanation given, shares in that arm of the company have plummeted. Bad news, yes?

ALEX: Yes.

MACK: Yes.

SCENIC: One would think so. Yes.

SUZANNE: Except, of course, for those who sold their shares just before they crashed. But I'm not here for that. For those who have made a killing, that's fine. They will have to hope there isn't an investigation into insider trading. They are no doubt buying back the shares right now at rock bottom to sell when the market reverses again. Which it will. And you know it will. Because you knew they would send someone like me to get you out of the hole you've dug yourselves into. I'm here to put Fellatio – which ever way you like it – back in the boudoirs of very household of this country.

SCENIC: Was that irony?

MACK: She's an American. She doesn't do irony.

SCENIC: Oh, yes. Of course.

ALEX: She comes from Canada. You'll upset her if you keep saying that.

MACK: Sorry, Ms.

SCENIC: Yes, Ms, do you know any Mounties?

SUZANNE: [*sigh*] I'm married to one.

MACK: Really? Do you ride together?

SUZANNE: Of course.

SCENIC: Reverse cowgirl?

SUZANNE: Possibly. And before you ask, my lover's a lumberjack. OK?

MACK: Really, Ms?

SCENIC: Do you perform fellatio with him, Ms?

MACK: Does he...

SCENIC: No. She can't. She's like this bottle of ginger ale.

ALEX: Schwepps...?

SCENIC: No. Canada Dry.

SUZANNE: OK. That's it. That's enough. Enough of your pathetic, puerile schoolyard humour. I can close this department down, you know. One click of my fingers and you're all history.

ALEX: Really?

MACK: We're impressed. Aren't we?

SCENIC: Keep it going Ms. I love a dominatrix. Especially a yank... sorry, a Can-nay-dee-an.

SUZANNE: Right: names. A new name. You have a piece of paper in front of you. We'll all write down a name for a brand new fragrance, fold them up and pass them to me. It'll be anonymous.

MACK: Oooh, a game! A game!

ALEX: We love games.

SUZANNE: After we've read the first ones we'll vote off one and all chose one of the one's left.

ALEX: God this is fun!

MACK: This rocks!

SCENIC: This is democracy!

MACK: Done mine, Ms!

SUZANNE: Right. Don't say which is yours. Mix them up. First one: "Shag Me".

SCENIC: That's yours, Alex, isn't it? I know your style.

SUZANNE: Sssh! Next "Poppadom City Lights".

MACK: Guess who?

SUZANNE: Third: "Dominatrix". And fourth: "Extra".

ALEX: Extra?

MACK: How crap is that?

SCENIC: Who's was that?

ALEX: Not mine – "Shag Me", right?

MACK: I was "Poppadom City Lights"

SCENIC: Of course. And I was "Dominatrix".

ALEX: So "Extra" must be Ms's.

SUZANNE: Well, I think… for a fragrance… a new one that has to appeal…

SCENIC: It's shite, Ms. I vote it off.

MACK: Me too.

ALEX: And me.

SUZANNE: Now look...

ALEX: It's all right! New game, first round demo. You can have another go!

SCENIC: But I want to read them out this time.

SUZANNE: OK.

*Ad lib as all write and pass papers to **Scenic** who reads each one and screws up paper and chucks it away.*

SCENIC: [*as if doing the Lottery draw*] OK. So we have, number one: "No, I really mean it: Shag Me!"

ALEX: [*giggles*]

SCENIC: Number two: "Poppadom City *Sights*";

MACK: I was gonna say "Shites" but I thought "Sights" was more appropriate.

SCENIC: Third one: "Cunny Lingers"; and – wait for it: finally "Klutzy".

SUZANNE: Hey wait a minute – I didn't... mine wasn't...

SCENIC: [*showing*] It's what it says here.

MACK: Yep. It does.

ALEX: Yep.

SCENIC: I like that. Well done Ms. I vote for "Klutzy".

MACK: Me too.

ALEX: And me.

SCENIC: Ms...? You're abstaining. Noble sentiment – shouldn't vote for yourself. That's it then. The new fragrance is Klutzy! A name thought up by our very own Ms. Suzanne the American...

ALEX: ...Canadian...

SCENIC: ...Can-nay-dee-an...

MACK: From China.

SUZANNE: [*packing up*] OK. Play it your own way. I shall deliver my report immediately to Sir John.

SCENIC: Sir John?

SUZANNE: Sir John Clitheroe, Owner and Chief Executive of this organisation. Recommendation: immediate closure of this department. So that there is no confusion let me just check your full names. Alexandra Channon?

ALEX: Yes, Ms.

SUZANNE: And John Macdonald?

MACK: Yes, Ms.

SUZANNE: And I don't have one for you, Mr. Route. Or "Rowt" as the Americans would say.

SCENIC: Is that Irony?

SUZANNE: It's a moot point. Well?

SCENIC: You almost made a joke there, Ms. I'm Jason, Ms. We're very sorry if we've upset you. Aren't we?

ALEX: Yes, we are. Really.

MACK: Yes, honest, we are. We'll be good now, promise.

ALEX: No more messing about.

SCENIC: We were only playing. Will you forgive us? Please?

SUZANNE: It's too late for that. Playtime has finished. For good. Full name?

SCENIC: Jason Clitheroe.

SUZANNE: Right. It's been interesting meeting you. I probably won't see you later.

> *Suzanne* exits. The others whistle, sing, play around a bit, paper planes etc.

> *Suzanne* returns. Silence.

SUZANNE: Did you say "Clitheroe"?

SCENIC: Yes, Ms. Jason. Jason Clitheroe.

SUZANNE: Are you…

SCENIC: Yes. He's my dad.

MACK: The Boss.

ALEX: The Owner. It's his firm.

MACK: Built it up from nothing, he did.

SCENIC: That's a moot point.

SUZANNE: [*clearing throat*] Right. I see. That puts... [*sitting*] Could I just say that, although it was, apparently, my suggestion, I'm not sure that "Klutzy" is the right choice for the new fragrance.

SCENIC: That's a moot point, Suzanne.

Blackout.

They Never Say Fuck On The Archers

```
They Never Say Fuck On
The Archers
by   Peter Yates
```
©COPYRIGHT 2008 Peter Yates

First Published 2009 by Random Cactus
ISBN 978-0-9559924-1-4

Rights of Performance are controlled by:

Random Cactus

New Place, Romeland Hill, St. Albans,

Herts. AL3 4ET

Phone: 01727 838540

Fax: 01727 843540

Email: random_cactus@yahoo.co.uk

Web: www.randomcactus.co.uk

 from whom a license for performance should be obtained.

It is an infringement of the Copyright to give any performance or public reading of the play before the license has been issued.

Characters:

Dave

Jessicca

A venue.

Dave is speaking into a microphone.

DAVE: Testing... testing... one... two... testing... one   two. Tes-ting ... er... bollocks. Bollocks. Bol-locks. Testing... one... two... shit. Sh - itt. Pisssss. Shittt. Bollocks. Bol-locks. One... two... Shit... piss... bollocks. Fuck. Fu-ckk.   Fuck. Testing. Fuck. Cu...

JESSICCA: I say!

DAVE: What...?

JESS: What do you think you are doing?

DAVE: Er... testing.... One... two ...

JESS: You know you can be heard out in the Foyer?

DAVE: Fuck!

JESS: Please! Desist. There are elderly people out there. And children. Very young children.

DAVE: Fuck! Sorry. I'll switch off.

JESS: Please do.

DAVE: Someone should have told me. That it's linked. To the Foyer speakers. I didn't know. Honest. No-one told me.

JESS: Well perhaps you should have checked.

DAVE: Ah. Yes. The perfect world eh?

JESS: What?

DAVE: In a perfect world... you know? In a perfect world there would be a white Christmas. In a perfect world there would be free beer on Saturdays. In a perfect world there would be two of me doing this. One out in the foyer, listening. The other in here saying shit... fuck... piss.

JESS: One is quite enough. Please don't use that sort of language. This is, after all, a conference for CAGWer

DAVE: I'm sorry?

JESS: CAGWer. Christians Against Global Warming.

DAVE: Is it..?

JESS: Yes.

DAVE: I didn't know that.

JESS: Well you do now.

DAVE: Well, fuck me.

JESS: Excuse me?

DAVE: No – you excuse me. Excuse my French in fact.

JESS: I'll leave you to your work. Please mind your language and if that proves to be impossible ensure that the relay to the foyer is disconnected.

DAVE: As you wish. [*pause*] Isn't that a bit of a contradiction in terms?

JESS: I'm sorry?

DAVE: CAGWer. Christians Against Global Warming?

JESS: I don't follow.

DAVE: Well, you're a Christian, right?

JESS: Right.

DAVE: And you believe in God, right?

JESS: Yes.

DAVE: And God created the world, right?

JESS: Well… yes…

DAVE: Slightly hesitant there, I feel. You're not an evolutionist, are you?

JESS: No.

DAVE: So God created man...

JESS: And woman.

DAVE: I was merely using "man" as a catch-all collective noun for humanity, really.

JESS: Well, perhaps you should use "woman" as a catch-all collective noun for humanity.

DAVE: Right. OK. But I'm just getting up to take-off speed on God and Global Warming so can we save the feminist debate for later?

JESS: As you wish.

DAVE: And God created m... the human race.

JESS: That's better.

DAVE: And humans are responsible for spewing out shed-loads of greenhouse gasses...

JESS: You can revert to just man for that one.

DAVE: Oooh! Do I detect a smidgen of a sense of humour beneath that rather superior exterior?

JESS: Finish your point.

DAVE: Well if God created the world and the human race and was pleased with what he created as we are told in the Bible, then he also created Global Warming so maybe its deliberate, maybe Global Warming is the Fifth Horseman of the Apocalypse and maybe this is it, this is the end of the world, maybe God wasn't quite so pleased and maybe the inevitable result of Global Warming is the biggest mega-fucking Armageddon that blows us all to kingdom-fucking-come and good old God can start all over again. [*Pause*] So. Christians, in theory, should be FOR global warming. Not against. 'Cos God created it. [*Pause*] It's just a thought.

JESS: You know, for a moment there, just a moment, I thought you were gong to get through your argument, make your point, a fair point even, without having to resort to the use of profanity. But no. Not a chance. It's ingrained. Like reality TV it permeates our being, devalues our *raison d'être* and cheapens our society. Had you made it through to the end without relapsing then I might well have been prepared to discuss the point with you. But… no. I don't think so.

DAVE: Don't you think I'm serious?

JESS: If you're serious come and speak at our conference.

DAVE: Do I get paid?

JESS: Oh, so mercenary.

DAVE: I'm freelance. If I come and speak for an hour at your conference then I'm losing an hour's pay from something else.

JESS: I doubt you'd last more than three minutes.

DAVE: Oooh. So harsh, from a Christian as well. Well... I'd lose three minute's pay... And there'd be questions wouldn't here? You'd need me to take questions from the floor.

JESS: Well since we've established you can't even do three minutes without swearing perhaps it's not such a good idea. It was nice meeting you...er...

DAVE: Dave.

JESS: It was nice meeting you David but I must get on.

DAVE: Dave, please. And you are...?

JESS: Jessica Robens.

DAVE: Mrs...?

JESS: Miss.

DAVE: So, Jess, do you never swear?

JESS: Jessica, please. Never

DAVE: Never?

JESS: Never.

DAVE: Not even inside your head?

JESS: No!

DAVE: Don't you ever go... you know... when something goes wildly wrong... like, well, you drop a yoghourt carton and the lid splits and it goes everywhere... don't you go... you know... in your head... don't you go: Oh, fuck?

JESS: No.

DAVE: Oh. Really?

JESS: Really.

DAVE: What do you say, then? In your head?

JESS: I say: silly yoghourt.

DAVE: Silly yoghourt?

JESS: Yes. Silly Yoghourt. You should try it.

DAVE: OK [*switches on mike*] Testing. Testing. One. Two. Silly yoghourt. Nah. Hasn't got the same ring to it. So in your whole life you've never ever said any kind of swear word ever at all, ever?

JESS: Well. If I'm absolutely honest, there was one I used to say. Quite a lot. When I was younger. It used to upset my mother. It was really quite naughty. She said they never used such language on Radio 4.

DAVE: Well come on, Jess. Jessica. I'm all ears.

JESS: I don't say it any more.

DAVE: There's no-one here. You can tell me. Go on. Be a devil.

JESS: Er-hem.

DAVE: Sorry. Be a little pixie-elf.

JESS: Knickers.

DAVE: [*through mike*] Knickers!

JESS: Sssshhh!

DAVE: You little dev...pixie-elf! You're telling me that you used to go around saying knickers. I'm shocked. Deeply shocked.

JESS: The point is I stopped saying it. I don't say it any more.

DAVE: You just did.

JESS: And you could stop swearing if you put your mind to it.

DAVE: It's funny isn't it – knickers sounds vaguely naughty - but not panties. People don't say: Oh, panties! Or thongs for that matter. When they drop the yoghourt hey don't say: Oh thongs! Hasn't got the same ring to it. So what do you wear? Knickers? Or panties? Or thongs.

JESS: What…?

DAVE: Sorry. Just the usual male-testosterone-fuelled idle interest.

JESS: Well you can f…

DAVE: You almost said it! You were gong to say it! You were going to tell me to fuck off!

JESS: I wasn't. I wasn't at all. I was going to say…. you can… forget it.

DAVE: A likely story. So you have never said fuck once in you whole life?

JESS: No. Never.

DAVE: Wouldn't you like to? Try it I mean? Just once.

JESS: No, I wouldn't.

DAVE: Come on. Lighten up. Chill. You're standing here, in your thong...

JESS: I am not wearing a th... one of those...

DAVE: Ah. Narrowed it down to two then.

JESS: Oh, you're impossible

DAVE: I'll tell you what. After the gig, we'll go out to dinner. Yes? Together. You and me. I'll pay – unless I can get through the whole meal without swearing – then you pay. Deal?

JESS: Is this...er... are you inviting me on a kind of date...?

DAVE: Yes. That's it. A date.

JESS: Sorry, David. Dave. I never date fuck-wits. [*exit*]

DAVE: What..? [*pause*] Testing. Testing. One. Two. Three. Knickers. Kni-ckers. Panties Pant-ies. Thongs. Nah. Hasn't got the same ring to it. Can you hear me in the foyer? Silly yoghourt …

<u>Blackout.</u>

Chance Meeting

Chance Meeting

by Peter Yates

©COPYRIGHT 2006 Peter Yates

First Published 2009 by Random Cactus
ISBN 978-0-9559924-1-4

Rights of Performance are controlled by:

Random Cactus

New Place, Romeland Hill, St. Albans,

Herts. AL3 4ET

Phone: 01727 838540

Fax: 01727 843540

Email: random_cactus@yahoo.co.uk

Web: www.randomcactus.co.uk

from whom a license for performance should be obtained.

It is an infringement of the Copyright to give any performance or public reading of the play before the license has been issued.

Characters:

Dudley

Babs

A street.

> ***Dudley*** *and **Babs** enter from opposite sides and immediately greet each other enthusiastically – hand-shake, kiss on cheek.*

BABS: Hi!

DUDLEY: Hello!

BABS: How are you?

DUDLEY: Good. How are you?

BABS: I'm good, good.

DUDLEY: Good. Good to see you.

BABS: You too. Good to see you, too. It's been…

DUDLEY: It's been a while!

BABS: Yes. It has. A while, yes. Probably… I don't know…

DUDLEY: No. It's amazing how the time flies, eh?

BABS: Yeah. Shocking. One day the kids are in nappies, next day they're doing their GCSE's.

DUDLEY: Or A levels even. University.

BABS: It just goes like that. [*snapping fingers*]

DUDLEY: In a flash. Yes. How are… the children…?

BABS: Fine, yes, fine. They're doing fine.

DUDLEY: Er… your…

BABS: …daughter…

DUDLEY: …is… how old is she now…?

BABS: Zoë?

DUDLEY: Of course. Zoë.

BABS: She's sixteen, going on twenty-one, know what I mean?

DUDLEY: Oh, yes, do I know what you mean. Been there. Done that. Got the paternity suits...

BABS: Of course... because...

DUDLEY: ...Sophie...

BABS: ...yes, Sophie... must be...

DUDLEY: ...eighteen...

BABS: Really?

DUDLEY: ...going on thirty-five!

BABS: I bet.

DUDLEY: Oh, yes.

BABS: If she's anything like Zoë it's a different boy every week.

DUDLEY: Well, no actually. She's er... actually shacked up with a 52 year-old record executive and they live in a mansion in Weybridge.

BABS: Really? God - that really is ... still I suppose she's got security...

DUDLEY: Electric fences, CCTV, guard dogs...

BABS: Oh. So no money worries, anyway. You don't have to worry...

DUDLEY: One baby already, another on the way.

BABS: Oh, that's nice... I bet you dote...

DUDLEY: Never see them, really. Big Shot, he is. They're always on holiday in Mustique. [*pause*] Hope you have better luck with Zoë.

BABS: Well, actually, she's studying for her GCSE's at home...

DUDLEY: Oh. Why's that, then?

BABS: You didn't hear? It *has* been along time!

DUDLEY: Ages.

BABS: She went and got herself pregnant. At fourteen.

DUDLEY: Really? I'm sorry… if that's the right…

BABS: No, no. You're all right. [*pause*] Just like me. Like mother, like daughter, eh?

DUDLEY: Yes… of course… I'd er… I hadn't actually realised…

BABS: So I'm a grandmother at 29.

DUDLEY: Shit.

BABS: Exactly.

DUDLEY: That's…er… that's er… really…

BABS: I know. You don't have to tell me. Still…

DUDLEY: Yes... I suppose there's always...

BABS: Her brother?

DUDLEY: Yes.

BABS: Gavin?

DUDLEY: Yes, Gavin. Of course. Now, how's he doing? How's Gavin?

BABS: He's got another ASBO

DUDLEY: Ah.

BABS: He won't go to school, ever.

DUDLEY: Oh, dear.

BABS: If he goes, he won't stay.

DUDLEY: I see.

BABS: Or he slags off the teachers.

DUDLEY:	Right.
BABS:	Or bullies the other kids.
DUDLEY:	Difficult.
BABS:	Got caught with a knife.
DUDLEY:	Oh, no…
BABS:	What are we meant to do? Where did we go wrong?
DUDLEY:	You and…
BABS:	His father. You know his father has tried everything.
DUDLEY:	Yes… er…
BABS:	He'll end up in prison. I mean, where does that come from, eh? He doesn't get it from us.
DUDLEY:	No. No. I can see that. It's obvious. Not from you and… er… how is er…

BABS: Geoff.

DUDLEY: Yes, Geoff. Of course. Geoff… still working at…

BABS: The factory. Yes. Promoted.

DUDLEY: Really?

BABS: Yes. Line Manager now.

DUDLEY: Now that *is* good.

BABS: He's a good man…

DUDLEY: Yes, yes, he is indeed…

BABS: A good husband.

DUDLEY: Yes. Yes.

BABS: Stood by me.

DUDLEY: Good. Yes. Er…

BABS: Despite the affair.

DUDLEY: Really? Now that is good.

BABS: Forgave me. Completely.

DUDLEY: Excellent.

BABS: Never mentions it.

DUDLEY: Fine. Fine. A good man.

BABS: And a good father. To Gavin.

DUDLEY: Yes. And look how he repays him.

BABS: Exactly.

DUDLEY: Still. Geoff is a good bloke. Good husband. Good father. To Gavin. And Zoë.

BABS: Oh, no, no. Not to Zoë. Never had any time for her.

DUDLEY: Oh, really? Sorry...

BABS: Not his, you see.

DUDLEY: Oh, I see...

BABS: Could never get past that.

DUDLEY: No, I can see that. I can see how that might be. Difficult...

BABS: Still, can't blame him, can we?

DUDLEY: No. I suppose we can't. Er... who...

BABS: Is the father? Of Zoë's child? The same bloke I had an affair with.

DUDLEY: Ah!

BABS: And who is also Zoë's father.

DUDLEY: Oh, my goodness.

BABS: You see...

DUDLEY: Oh, yes. I see. I can quite see where Geoff is coming from.

Pause.

BABS: What about...

DUDLEY: Celia? She's gone back into teaching.

BABS: Oh that's nice.

DUDLEY: Yes. She hates it.

BABS: Ah.

DUDLEY: Bureaucracy. Red Tape. Filling in forms. "When am I going to get to see a class of kids?" she screams.

BABS: Terrible, isn't it? That's the Government for you.

DUDLEY: Then when she does get to teach there's always some little brat who takes pleasure in slagging her off.

BABS: Oh. I see. Like…

DUDLEY: Oh, no, no! I didn't mean…

BABS: No. It's OK. I know you didn't… Couldn't she…

DUDLEY: No. Not really. It's the money. We need the money.

BABS: Right. Yes. Of course. Er… for your…

DUDLEY: …son…?

BABS: Yes, your son…

DUDLEY: George.

BABS: Of course.

DUDLEY: That's it, you see. George. Never done a day's work since he left Uni. 24 he is.

BABS: At least he got a degree…

DUDLEY: Left, did I say? Thrown out.

BABS: Ah.

DUDLEY: Didn't do any work there, either.

BABS: No. He's a teeny bit lazy…

DUDLEY: Sits on the sofa all day. Watching daytime TV.

BABS: That's all rubbish, isn't it?

DUDLEY: Won't look for a job. Doesn't want to work.

BABS: Right. Now that's a problem, isn't it?

DUDLEY: And the rehab costs a fortune.

BABS: Of course.

DUDLEY: And he keeps absconding.

BABS: Oh, dear.

DUDLEY: Has to start again. Every time.

BABS: I see. Yes. Expensive.

DUDLEY: Very, very expensive. It's a nightmare.

BABS: He's… er… still kind of addicted to er…

DUDLEY: Heroin.

BABS: Oooh. Nasty.

DUDLEY: Coke. Crack. Pills. Pot. Crystal Meth. You name it.

BABS: I couldn't. I don't understand it. Gavin's not like that, fortunately.

DUDLEY: No?

BABS: No. He just sells them. Hence the ASBO.

DUDLEY: Right. [*pause*] Tragedy. George. Complete tragedy.

BABS: Yeah. I can see that. Yeah. Must be...

DUDLEY: Yeah. It is.

BABS: Couldn't you ...

DUDLEY: Ask the Big Shot for some cash?

BABS: Well it's a thought.

DUDLEY: No. No way. Never. Not even if I ... well... say... not even if I couldn't afford a tank of petrol. There is no way I'm going cap in hand...

BABS: No, well, I can understand...

DUDLEY: He's the one that got George hooked in the first place.

BABS: Ah.

DUDLEY: And Sophie.

BABS: Oh.

DUDLEY: Probably the kid by now too.

BABS: Oh dear. And…

DUDLEY: Yeah, you're right. Probably the next one's weaned onto it as well. Criminal. That's what it is. Criminal.

BABS: They don't care, do they? Don't think about the consequences.

DUDLEY: Selfishness. That's what it is. Pure selfishness.

BABS: Self, self, self. That's all they think about.

DUDLEY: You are not wrong about that. Record Executive, did I say?

BABS: Well…

DUDLEY: Record Executive my arse! He runs the country's biggest drugs smuggling organisation.

BABS: Is that right?

DUDLEY: The music business: the perfect cover.

BABS: Yes, I suppose so.

DUDLEY: He's just another sleaze-ball drug-runner living on the proceeds of other people's misery. Like poor George.

BABS: Well I suppose technically Sophie is as well.

DUDLEY: What...?

BABS: Well... I didn't mean... I meant... you know, the CCTV cameras and...

DUDLEY: No – you're so right. I hadn't really thought that one through. Sophie is living the high life off of her brother's misery.

BABS: Well... I was only saying...

DUDLEY: Thank you. You have opened my eyes for me.

BABS: Well... glad to have been...

DUDLEY: When I see Sophie next…

BABS: Yes…

DUDLEY: <u>If</u> I see Sophie next…

BABS: Yes!

DUDLEY: I shall give her a piece of my mind! I shall tell her that a…

BABS: …an acquaintance…

DUDLEY: I shall tell her that… a friend…

BABS: Thank you.

DUDLEY: A friend… has opened my eyes to the real cost to her brother of shagging a Big Shot international criminal mastermind.

BABS: That'll tell her.

DUDLEY: Thank you. This is quite cathartic.

BABS: Yes. For me too. [*pause*] Cathartic…?

DUDLEY: Purgative…?

BABS: Huh…?

DUDLEY: Releasing, freeing. Relieving the tension. The stress.

BABS: Don't talk to me about stress.

DUDLEY: No…?

BABS: Well, after I had the melanoma removed – obviously I'd lost all my hair because of the chemo…

DUDLEY: Obviously…

BABS: …well they said it had been successful…

DUDLEY: Good…

BABS: But then I got a letter saying that there'd been some foul up at the hospital…

DUDLEY: Oh, no…

BABS: Samples, you know, something had got mixed up…

DUDLEY: How appalling…

BABS: Surgical instruments not sterilised properly…

DUDLEY: You can sue you know.

BABS: And the upshot is I might have something or I might not, they don't know, they have to do these tests, they have to do those tests, and I'm still waiting for the results.

DUDLEY: I can see why you're stressed!

BABS: So I'm just kind of in limbo, really, waiting…

DUDLEY: You can treat stress, you know. Get it treated. Celia...

BABS: Celia's suffering from it too...?

DUDLEY: Yes. I'm afraid so. Down to me really.

BABS: Oh...?

DUDLEY: Yes. When I came out.

BABS: Came... out...?

DUDLEY: Of the closet.

BABS: The clos... Oh. Yes, I can see...

DUDLEY: Yes.

Pause.

DUDLEY: Anyway. I suppose I'd better be getting along.

BABS: Yeah. Me too. Got to pick up my grand daughter...

DUDLEY: Wish I could say the same thing.

BABS: Yes. Sorry. [*pause*] OK, er...

DUDLEY: Dudley.

BABS: Babs. [*pause*] Where is it you know me from?

DUDLEY: Er... I don't. I thought you knew me.

BABS: Well you seem very familiar.

DUDLEY: You too.

BABS: Do you er... live round here?

DUDLEY: South of the river.

BABS: North of the river.

DUDLEY: Not kids schools, then.

BABS: No. Work?

DUDLEY/BABS: No.

BABS: Holiday perhaps. Ibiza?

DUDLEY: Never been there. Skiathos?

BABS: Where's that?

DUDLEY: A Greek Island.

BABS: Ah. No. Well…

DUDLEY: I'm struggling here…

BABS: Me too.

DUDLEY: I don't think I've ever met you before.

BABS: No. I think you're right. I've never met <u>you</u> before. Still it's been nice…

DUDLEY: No, very nice. Very pleasant talking to you.

BABS: You too.

DUDLEY: Good luck with...

BABS: Gavin's ASBO. Thanks. I hope that...

DUDLEY: Sophie leaves the Big Shot. Yeah, me too. And tell Zoë...

BABS: To keep her legs together. Right. And I hope that...

DUDLEY: George gets clean and stays clean. So do I. Thanks for your concern.

BABS: And you.

DUDLEY: Well. Maybe we'll meet...

BABS: ...again...

DUDLEY: ...maybe...

BABS: I'd like that.

DUDLEY: Get an update.

BABS: Yes. That would be good.

Babs's mobile rings.

BABS: Excuse me. Hello, love. Everything OK? Ah.

Holds mobile away from mouth.

BABS: [*to* **Dudley**, *stage whisper*] Gavin's been arrested. [*into mobile*] So… what was that love…?

Holds mobile away from mouth.

BABS: [*to* **Dudley**, *stage whisper*] And Zoë's expecting. Again. [*into mobile*] OK, love. We'll talk about it later. I'll be back soon. Shall I pick up something nice for tea? OK, then. 'Bye.

Dudley's Mobile rings.

DUDLEY: Hello, Cee. Everything all right? Huh? Oh dear.

Holds mobile away from mouth.

DUDLEY: George is in a coma. Overdose. [*into mobile*] Don't worry, Cee. I'll get there as soon as possible. Which hospital? What was that?

Holds mobile away from mouth.

DUDLEY: Big Shot's dumped Sophie. She's threatening to jump off a multi-storey. With the kid. [*into mobile*] OK, Cee. Calm down. Please. You're getting hysterical. Leave it to the Police. The Police are trained... She hung up.

BABS: Ah.

Pause.

DUDLEY: Babs, do you fancy...

BABS: Er... what, Dudley...?

DUDLEY: I just wondered if you fancied...

***Babs's** mobile rings.*

BABS: Oops! Sorry. Hello? Who's that? The hospital? Ah. I see. Ah you certain about that? Oh.

Holds mobile away from mouth.

BABS: Tests have come through. I've got Hepatitis C. [*into mobile*] Thank you for calling to let me know. 'Bye. Sorry, Dudley. What were you saying?

DUDLEY: I'm so sorry, Babs, to hear…

BABS: It's OK, Dudley. No big deal. You were asking if I fancied…

Dudley's *mobile rings.*

DUDLEY: Sorry. Hello. Ah, yes, that's me. Who…? The Clinic? Ah, I see.

Holds mobile away from mouth.

DUDLEY: I'm HIV positive. [*into mobile*] You sure there's not been a mistake? OK. Thank you. Thanks for calling.

BABS: Dudley...

DUDLEY: No worries. It was on the cards. No, Babs, I was just wondering if you fancied...

BABS: A nice cup of tea?

DUDLEY: Yes!

BABS: Oh. Yes. Definitely.

They both look at mobiles. Switch them off.

DUDLEY: Off?

BABS: Off.

And exit.

<u>Blackout.</u>

Corkage

Corkage

by Peter Yates

©COPYRIGHT 2006 Peter Yates

First Published 2009 by Random Cactus
ISBN 978-0-9559924-1-4

Rights of Performance are controlled by:

Random Cactus

New Place, Romeland Hill, St. Albans,

Herts. AL3 4ET

Phone: 01727 838540

Fax: 01727 843540

Email: random_cactus@yahoo.co.uk

Web: www.randomcactus.co.uk

from whom a license for performance should be obtained.

It is an infringement of the Copyright to give any performance or public reading of the play before the license has been issued.

Characters:

Bob

Carol

Ted

Alice

A garden. A summer's evening.

***Bob** & **Carol** & **Ted** & **Alice** are sitting around a table, drinking wine.*

BOB: Ten pounds!

TED: How much?

CAROL: Ten pounds. It was actually ten pounds.

ALICE: What… a one off payment? That sounds pretty standard.

BOB: Per bottle.

TED/ALICE: What!

CAROL: Ten pounds per bottle. Every single bottle.

ALICE: How many bottles?

BOB: One hundred and twenty.

TED: One hundred and twenty?

ALICE: One hundred and twenty – bottles.

CAROL: One hundred and twenty.

TED: That's – one thousand two hundred pounds.

BOB/ CAROL: One thousand two hundred pounds.

TED: That's outrageous. Daylight robbery.

BOB: Tell me about it.

ALICE: So let me get this straight. You took…

CAROL: …one hundred and twenty…

ALICE: …bottles…

TED: …of Champagne…

CAROL: …to the hotel.

BOB: Our own champagne...

CAROL: ...which we bought cheap...

BOB: ...off a mate of mine...

CAROL: ...in a pub.

BOB: Took them into the hotel...

TED: Five star hotel...

BOB: Very posh, very plush, five star hotel...

CAROL: ...for the wedding reception.

BOB: Our daughter.

CAROL: She looked lovely in the white with the bright pink trim.

BOB: Clashed violently with the bridesmaids' greengage.

CAROL: That's a matter of opinion.

TED: One hundred and twenty bottles of your own champagne…

CAROL: And they…

BOB/CAROL/TED/ALICE: …charged ten pounds a bottle.

TED: One thousand two hundred pounds.

CAROL: Ten pounds a bottle.

BOB: Corkage.

TED: That's right. Corkage

CAROL: Corkage.

ALICE: Corkage.

TED: They can do that, you see.

CAROL: Yes they can. They can do that.

BOB: You can't stop them. They've got you over a barrel.

TED: What - a barrel of wine?

Laugh.

BOB: They're holding a gun to your head. You can't say no because they'll pull the plug on the whole shooting match.

TED: And the wine will all flow out through the plug-hole!

Laugh.

BOB: It's Corporate Hospitality blackmail, basically. That's what it is.

TED: Or wine mail.

No laugh.

BOB/CAROL: What?

TED: Nothing.

Pause.

ALICE: What is corkage?

BOB/CAROL/TED: What?

ALICE: What actually is corkage? I've heard the expression but what is it actually? What does it do? How does it work? Why does it cost one thousand two hundred quid, for heaven's sake?

TED: Steady on, dear.

BOB: Corkage is a levy exacted by the host establishment for the extraction by the host establishment's catering staff of the cork in the neck of the bottle of wine which is in place to ensure the preservation of the wine so that the drinker of the beverage can enjoy the optimum condition of the said wine on drinking.

ALICE: What?

TED: Pulling the cork out the bottle.

ALICE: Oh. I see. And they charge?

BOB/CAROL/TED: Ten pounds a bottle.

ALICE: Ten pounds a bottle?

CAROL: One hundred and twenty bottles.

ALICE: One hundred and twenty bottles?

TED: One thousand two hundred pounds.

ALICE: One thousand two hundred... that's daylight robbery...

BOB: Yes.

ALICE: Daylight robbery

CAROL: That's right.

ALICE: Is that what corkage is?

TED: Yes.

ALICE: That's outrageous. I never knew that's what corkage was. Why do people pay it?

BOB: Got you over a barrel.

CAROL: They put a gun to your head.

TED: Corporate Hospitality blackmail.

ALICE: Oh. Right. So you had to pay one thousand…

BOB/ CAROL: No!

TED: No?

BOB: That's just it. We didn't!

ALICE: What – didn't pay corkage?

CAROL: No!

ALICE: But I thought you said…

BOB: They <u>imposed</u> corkage...

CAROL: But we didn't pay it.

TED: How come?

BOB: Well. That's the clever bit.

CAROL: Yeah, listen to this. Hear what Bob did. This really is clever. Isn't it Bob?

BOB: Well, I suppose, all modesty aside, it was just a teeny bit clever.

CAROL: A teeny bit? It was massively clever. It was really clever. It was really, really clever. You just listen to this. Listen to what Bob did.

ALICE: Well, yes, we'd like to.

BOB: Well, you see...

CAROL: Oh this is so funny this is. You just listen to this. I almost wet myself laughing when he tells this. It is so clever.

TED/ALICE: Really?

CAROL: Oh yes, yes, really. Tell them, Bob.

ALICE: Yeah, do tell us Bob.

BOB: OK, Alice, what I did was this…

*Shrieks from **Carol**.*

BOB: Yes, OK Carol, calm down dear it's not that funny.

CAROL: Oh, yes it is! And clever. You listen to this Alice…

ALICE: Well, yes I'm, trying to.

BOB: Well what I did was…

CAROL: This is what he did.

BOB: I picked on the most junior employee of the catering staff…

CAROL: A spotty young kid just out of school.

BOB: Work experience.

ALICE: Oh, yes?

CAROL: It was his first day.

TED: Oh, right.

BOB: Anyway…

CAROL: Tell them what you did, Bob.

BOB: I will, Carol, give me a chance, OK?

CAROL: This is so clever, Ted, you just listen…

BOB: I said to this kid, I said, what's your name?

CAROL: He did…

BOB: And he said, Matthew. And I said…

CAROL: Bob said...

BOB: Matthew? That's the same name as our son.

ALICE: Is it?

CAROL: No.

ALICE: That's what I thought. Your son is Mark...

CAROL: Marcus.

ALICE: That's what I thought. Not Matthew. So why did you say...

TED: To get his confidence, am I right?

BOB/CAROL: Yes!

TED: Now, hush up, Alice and listen.

ALICE: Sorry.

BOB: I said to him, Matthew, I said...

CAROL: ...Matthew, he said...

BOB: Matthew, have you got your bottle opener handy? And Matthew says: Yes, sir, I have sir. Here it is, sir!

CAROL: Here it is, sir!

BOB: So I said to him...

CAROL: This is the really clever bit...

BOB: I said to him: Matthew, it would be a great help to us if you could go round and open up all these bottles beforehand so that there's no delay when the guests come in. So he said...

CAROL: Listen to what he said...

ALICE: What did he say, Bob?

TED: Sssh!

BOB: He said, Matthew said: Right, sir. Of course, sir. And he grabs a bottle...

CAROL: All the other caterers are in the next room...

BOB: He grabs a bottle...

TED: What, a Champagne bottle...?

BOB: He grabs a Champagne bottle...

CAROL: Champagne bottle...

BOB: ...and starts putting his cork-screw into it!

TED: A Champagne bottle!

CAROL: Yes, Ted, a Champagne bottle!

ALICE: What's wrong with that?

TED: You don't open Champagne bottles with a corkscrew, do you...

CAROL: Alice.

TED: Push and pop!

ALICE: Oh yes, of course, I see! So he was putting...

CAROL: A cork-screw...

BOB/TED: In a Champagne bottle!

CAROL: We don't know what to do with ourselves by now.

BOB: We are just creasing up!

CAROL: Choking with laughter...

They laugh.

TED: So... what happened?

BOB: After a bit he comes over to me and says...

CAROL: This is what he says, this Matthew guy...

BOB: He says: Excuse me sir, please don't tell my boss…

CAROL: Don't tell my boss…

ALICE: Oh, sweet, don't tell…

TED: …his boss.

BOB: But I don't seem to be making much headway with this cork!

TED: Priceless!

ALICE: Right. He's putting the cork-screw into the Champagne cork…

TED: Exactly!

CAROL: So Bob says…

BOB: I say: Probably a dud cork. Try another one.

CAROL: Try another one!

ALICE: Try another one?

TED: Try another one!

BOB: So he does!

CAROL: He does!

BOB: And he keeps on trying them until he's done almost the whole lot.

TED: No!

CAROL: Yes!

TED: What a complete idiot.

CAROL: Complete fool.

BOB: So at this point the boss comes in...

CAROL: Bob feigns no knowledge of this...

TED: No...

CAROL: Yes!

BOB: And the boss comes over and says...

CAROL: I'm terribly sorry, sir, there seems...

BOB: ...to be a little problem.

ALICE: The boy's boss...

BOB: Oh, yes...?

CAROL: ...Bobs says in his sternest voice.

BOB: Oh, yes? This is my daughter's wedding.

BOB/ CAROL: I don't want any hitches.

TED: Hitches...?

CAROL: Yes, hitches!

ALICE: Hitches...

CAROL: Except for the bride and groom!

Laugh.

BOB: Well, we've had a little problem with the corkage, says the boss, all po-faced.

CAROL: The corkage? - we say.

BOB: Yes sir, but don't worry. We'll sort it out. And we won't charge you corkage.

CAROL: He's holding a bottle with a cork-screw sticking out!

TED: No!

CAROL: Yes!

BOB: I should hope not...

CAROL: Bob says.

BOB: In fact...

CAROL: Wait for this, this really is priceless.

BOB: As you appear to have destroyed all our champagne corks…

CAROL: Which we intended to give to our guests as souvenirs…

BOB: We will charge <u>you</u> corkage!

ALICE: And did you?

BOB/CAROL: We did!

TED: How much?

BOB: Ten pounds a bottle.

ALICE: Ten pounds a bottle!

CAROL: Ten pounds a bottle.

TED: Ten pounds a bottle. One hundred and twenty bottles?

BOB: One hundred and twenty bottles.

ALICE: One hundred and twenty bottles?

CAROL: One hundred and twenty bottles!

BOB: One thousand two hundred pounds off our bill!

TED: Fantastic!

ALICE: Amazing!

TED: What a scam!

ALICE: You showed them!

BOB: Had them over a barrel.

CAROL: Had a gun to their heads.

TED: Corporate Hospitality blackmail - in reverse!

ALICE: Brilliant!

Laugh.

TED: Here's to corkage!

BOB: Cheers! Corkage!

CAROL: Salut! Corkage!

ALICE: Corkage!

Pause.

ALICE: By the way, what did you say corkage was?

<u>Blackout</u>

First Casualty

First Casualty

by Peter Yates

©COPYRIGHT 2007 Peter Yates

First Published 2009 by Random Cactus
ISBN 978-0-9559924-1-4

Rights of Performance are controlled by:

Random Cactus

New Place, Romeland Hill, St. Albans,

Herts. AL3 4ET

Phone: 01727 838540

Fax: 01727 843540

Email: random_cactus@yahoo.co.uk

Web: www.randomcactus.co.uk

from whom a license for performance should be obtained.

It is an infringement of the Copyright to give any performance or public reading of the play before the license has been issued.

Characters:

Ryan

Eva

Cal

Morris

An Office. Somewhere, soon.

*Body on floor **dsr**. **Ryan** kneeling over it feeling for pulse. **Eva** and **Cal** standing, watching.*

EVA: Dead?

RYAN: Yes. Yes.

EVA: [*looking at **Cal***] How…?

CAL: How the fuck should I know?

Pause.

EVA: Close his eyelids.

CAL: Why?

EVA: That's what you do. When someone dies.

RYAN: You do it. It's not something I've er… ever had to…

EVA: Oh. I couldn't touch him.

Eva & Ryan look at Cal.

CAL: They'll stay open then.

Pause.

RYAN: Shouldn't we… shouldn't we…

CAL: Shouldn't we what?

EVA: Shouldn't we tell someone?

CAL: Who?

Eva looks at Ryan.

RYAN: I don't know.

CAL: [*offering 'phone*] You want to tell someone – tell someone.

Silence.

CAL: We'll put him in the corridor. Tonight. He'll be gone by morning.

EVA: Like Sebastian.

RYAN: Sebastian was killed.

CAL: And Morris died. What's the difference?

Pause.

EVA: Spooky. Having a dead person here. Someone who was living, talking, laughing with us just…

RYAN: [*sharply*] Give it a rest, Eva. [*softer*] Please. Sorry.

EVA: Sorry. Shouldn't we…

CAL: [*exploding*] Shouldn't we what?

EVA: Give him last rights… or something.

CAL: He's dead! Too fucking late!

EVA: Say a prayer? Cover him up?

CAL: [*dropping sheets of paper on the body*] Here lies Morris. Former advertising executive, lately tool of the State. He served his country well covering up the truth, telling lies and inventing all sorts of highly original propaganda. Perversely he was far better at that than he ever was at advertising – one might even venture that he finally discovered his true calling before his untimely death at the age of 39. We wish him peace and happiness in his new resting place as he has surely gone to meet his maker: Dr Paul Joseph Goebbels.

RYAN: Who?

CAL: You are an ignorant twat, Ryan, aren't you?

Ryan turns away. Pause. Ryan picks up some papers from table.

RYAN: OK. We'd better get on. These are Morris's notes. He must have made them last night. While we slept. Before…

CAL: Before he kicked the bucket.

Eva *turns away, trying not to cry.*

RYAN: Anyway, it gives us a good insight into his thinking about the current project. We've all been struggling with it…

CAL: Too right.

RYAN: But, if I'm reading these right, Morris had come up with a formula for cracking it.

EVA: Good. That's good isn't it Cal?

CAL: Go on.

RYAN: As we are all aware, our government has been using tactical nuclear weapons on several suspected terrorist bases in various locations near the theatre of war. We didn't know this, but Morris was specifically concerned with one of these bases in…

EVA: Ryan…

RYAN: Sorry.

CAL: We are not allowed to say place names, ever, in case we are being bugged.

RYAN: Sorry.

CAL: I say in case: of course we're being bugged. By their people. By our people. By God knows what other people. You <u>know</u> that.

EVA: He said he was sorry, Cal.

CAL: How many times...

RYAN: Morris never bothers about that...

CAL: Morris is dead. We can't hide behind him anymore. We go by the book. Now. You know the rules...

RYAN: [*sharply*] I said I'm sorry! OK? This is not an ordinary morning. This is not a normal working day. We are all under pressure. Today more than ever.

EVA: Write it down, Ryan.

Ryan writes on piece of paper and hands it to them.

RYAN: Reports have leaked out through the media which speculate about these detonations and hint at this [*indicating paper*] location but falling short from naming it. We have to come up with a strategy for presenting this to the public, in a form that will be palatable, should the need arise.

CAL: We know the need's going to arise. It always does. Morris wouldn't have known about it otherwise. It's all about need to know. They know full well they're going to need us. The Sultans of Spin.

EVA: [*reading*] He finishes this last note mid-sentence.

RYAN: Yeah...

EVA: He says: "The consumer reaction to this copy has negative likelihood i.e. widespread, violent and severely anti-client. We can nullify this by... it's one for us... I can't..."

CAL: Relevance?

RYAN: It's almost as if he...

CAL: [*turning away*] Oh, for fuck's sake!

EVA: I know, Ryan. I know what you're saying. It's as if... as if...

RYAN: Go on.

EVA: As if he couldn't bring himself to lie any more.

RYAN: And lost the will to live.

CAL: He wasn't lying! We don't lie. We just manipulate the truth.

EVA: Well...

CAL: Morris was the best. Morris <u>was</u> Mr. Propaganda. He was what made this unit a success. Sound-bite of the week 16 weeks in a row. Top Team Award month after month. Certificates, medals, trophies coming out of our ears. And the big one, Spin of the Year once again this spring. We're so good we get jeered at awards ceremonies. That was all Morris. All Morris. We lived off him, he was our meal ticket. He <u>was</u> the best. And he didn't want anyone dragging us down. Which is why he killed Sebastian.

RYAN: What?

EVA: Cal…

RYAN: No, Cal. Sebastian was killed by an intruder.

CAL: You see? Morris was the best. He could spin anything.

RYAN: Fuck.

EVA: Fuck.

CAL: Come on! We were all relieved when Sebastian was out of the frame. He held us back. When he went we really started to zing. Do you remember the Rations Fiasco?

RYAN: Oh, yes. That was priceless.

EVA: The Ministry of Defence giving dog meat to the troops at the front.

CAL: Morris working like he was on crystal meth or something. "Yes. The MOD is providing dog meat to our boys at the front. And grateful they are too! No, it is not just another cost-saving exercise. The layman" – great turn of phrase our Morris had – "will probably not be aware of a certain substance known as…

RYAN/EVA: Canine-derived seryatin!

CAL: …found in most animals but particularly prevalent in dogs…

EVA: ...that has been discovered...

RYAN: ...by our top scientists...

EVA: ...to contain anti-bodies that can counter the effect of mustard gas...

CAL: ...and other chemical agents". Brilliant!

RYAN: You have to hand it to old Morris. He was A1.

EVA: What about the equipment deficiencies?

RYAN: Soldiers dying because body armour was issued on a one-between-two basis.

CAL: And they had to toss a coin to see who would wear it that day. Morris was in his element.

EVA: The MOD was really on the rack about that one.

RYAN: The Government was ready to resign.

CAL: And then in the nick of time, Morris comes up with…

EVA: "The company that supplies the armour has been infiltrated…

RYAN: … by the enemy…

CAL: …they've sabotaged every second set…

RYAN: …by injecting Polonium…

EVA: …which is released when you tighten the straps.

CAL: So all the affected suits have been withdrawn…

RYAN: …and buried in concrete…

EVA: …which is why the troops are short…

CAL: …but a major annihilation of our boys has been averted".

RYAN: Overnight zero to hero for the Defence Minister.

EVA: Government praised for its vigilance and care.

CAL: The sacrifice of a couple of hundred soldiers, through lack of body armour, was a small price to pay.

RYAN: No-one dare attack foreign policy after that.

CAL: Well played, Morris.

RYAN: And what about the reasons for war?

CAL: That was his *pièce de resistance*.

EVA: Why have we gone to war with a distant country on the other side of the world?

RYAN: Particularly when other countries in the region have been drawn in and every terrorist organisation in the world has taken up this war – against us - as its *cause célèbre*.

CAL: We're shunned by the UN...

EVA: ...and for which we have no allies at all...

RYAN: ...even the United States turns around and says...

CAL: "It is not our policy to support an aggressor".

RYAN: So what does Morris come up with?

CAL: The tunnel.

EVA/RYAN: The tunnel.

CAL: The biggest fucking mind-blowingly long tunnel in the history of the universe.

EVA: Our enemies...

RYAN: ...on the other side of the world...

CAL: ...have started to dig a tunnel.

EVA: A big tunnel.

RYAN: A big, long tunnel.

CAL: A mega-fucking long tunnel for which they have a mega-fucking mahousive machine to gouge it out.

EVA: And it's going through the centre of the earth and coming out...

RYAN: In Cheltenham.

CAL: "You've heard of the China Syndrome", says Morris, "where a nuclear reactor in the US melts down and down until it comes out in China".

RYAN: This was to be The Cheltenham Syndrome, where our enemies on the other side of the world would burrow through and surface in that pretty little spa town known for its cream teas and racing festival. Millions of soldiers would come belching out, taking us by complete surprise and over-running the country.

EVA: As a pre-cursor to conquering Europe.

RYAN: And eventually the United States.

CAL: And a nervous, gullible, security-obsessed nation bought it. Granted you had a particularly plausible PM; granted you had computer models, mock-ups, cleverly constructed surveillance pictures and testimony from sources that were known to have impeccable credentials and had always been reliable in the past. And granted you had a flawless dossier, friends, put together by us, which left no scintilla of space for counter-argument.

EVA: So we went to war to stop the tunnel.

RYAN: Which, after four and a half years they still haven't found.

CAL: But we find it impossible to extricate ourselves from the conflict.

EVA: Which grows bloodier by the minute.

RYAN: And now we're using tactical nuclear weapons to try and bring it to a swift conclusion.

EVA: And the client tried very hard to keep <u>that</u> under wraps.

CAL: Which brings us back neatly to this day-urgent project. How do we sell <u>that</u> concept to the consumer?

RYAN: How would Morris have sold it?

CAL: Morris isn't here. Any more. We're on our own. But he's taught us all he knew.

EVA: We can't let him down.

RYAN: We must carry on his work.

CAL: His life must not have been in vain. So. Ideas.

Pause.

RYAN: It was an accident. The bombs went off by accident.

EVA: What were the bombs doing there anyway?

RYAN: They weren't our bombs. We...

CAL: Captured them?

RYAN: And they went off by accident.

CAL: Or they had been primed to go off by the enemy...

EVA: ...who allowed us to capture them.

Pause.

ALL: Nah.

Pause.

EVA: How about... nuclear devices were buried by the enemy to get our troops but our bombing set them off prematurely?

Pause.

CAL/RYAN: Nah.

Pause.

CAL: Wait a minute. This wasn't actually nuclear bombs at all but - a large rogue asteroid that collided with earth?

RYAN: And everyone's attention was on the war so no-one noticed its progress?

CAL: Yeah, possibly.

RYAN: There is evidence of asteroids landing in that region before.

CAL: We could say we're in the middle of a major asteroid storm and they'll be others hitting earth - and we could

	stage one in somewhere like, I don't know, Essex?
EVA:	Put out scientific data proving that some of the fissile material in asteroids is nuclear.
RYAN:	Or even... this was a manufactured nuclear meteor sent to earth by aliens!
CAL/ RYAN:	Yes!
	Pause.
ALL:	Nah.
CAL:	Oh. This is hopeless. How did Morris do it? He always instinctively knew exactly the right line to spin immediately with hardly any apparent thought.
RYAN:	Yeah, he'd tell us what it was and then we'd just spend as long as it took supplying evidence, data, interviews, comment - whatever was needed.
EVA:	It was great, wasn't it? Fun?

CAL: I loved it.

RYAN: Me too.

CAL: Yeah. I miss Morris already.

EVA: Poor Morris.

CAL: Look, we have a deadline on this. We're getting nowhere. We'll have to 'phone through and ask for help from other departments.

All nod agreement. **Cal** *goes to desk and picks up 'phone.*

MOR: [*sitting up*] Other departments! What the fuck are you talking about?

EVA: Morris... you're not...

RYAN: ...dead.

MOR: Rumours of my demise appear to have been spun out of all fucking proportion. Of course I'm not dead!

CAL: Thank God! Morris, we've got a real problem with this tactical nuclear weapons thing.

MOR: Can't leave you alone for a couple of hours without you going excremental. I really thought you'd be able to get the branding on this one. From my notes. Listen. Absorb. Envision your minds. Empower yourselves.

CAL: We... tried... we read your notes.

MOR: I heard. "We can counter this by... it's one for us..."

RYAN: Yes...

MOR: Not "us" you morons! U.S.

EVA: Of course! It's good to have you back, Morris. Just add water, guys.

CAL/RYAN: U.S.?

MOR: It's a no brainer: the tactical battlefield nuclear weapons used on terrorist training camps near the conflict currently involving our armed forces were deployed by: the United States of America.

RYAN: But the Americans aren't involved – they're not even our allies in this conflict.

MOR: That is their public position. But we shall say they have been helping us <u>covertly</u>.

CAL: But the Yanks will deny it.

MOR: Exactly. And, my friends, who will believe them?

Pause as it sinks in then ad lib laughs, congrats., hand-shakes, hugs etc. as lights fade to

<u>**Blackout.**</u>

Encounters With Doormen

epilogue

Epilogue.

> **Lobb** is standing in front of Club entrance. **Clubber** and **Girlfriend** enter from Club.

LOBB: Good night, sir, good night, madam.

GIRL: [*giggles*]

CLUBBER: Er... do you think I can have my trainers back, please? You took them off me on the way in.

LOBB: I'm afraid I can't do that, sir.

CLUBBER: Why's that?

LOBB: There was a strange odour emanating from them, sir. They thus constituted a possible threat to the public. We had to have a controlled detonation.

CLUBBER: What...?

LOBB: Might have been plastic explosive.

CLUBBER: You blew up my trainers?

GIRL: [giggles]

LOBB: Madam, may I enquire as to what you are holding.

GIRL: It's a plastic banana. Won it in the Karaoke competition.

LOBB: I'm afraid I will have to disarm you of that, madam.

GIRL: Disarm?

LOBB: It could constitute a danger to the public.

GIRL: Danger…?

Lobb snatches banana. Girl starts to cry.

GIRL: He stole my banana! He stole my banana!

CLUBBER: Well I hope you feel good about yourself. You've spoilt a good evening. Destroyed my trainers, nicked her banana. Is that it? Are we free to go? Anything else about my person you want to confiscate.

LOBB: Yes, sir. Seeing as you mention it. Your trousers.

CLUBBER: My what...?

LOBB: Trousers. They constitute a potential indictment of public disorder.

CLUBBER: "Incitement" not "indictment" you thick cockney twat.

LOBB: That's what I said sir. Indictment. And if you don't remove them [*holding up mobile camera 'phone*] your picture will be circulated to every doorman at...

LOBB/CLUBBER/GIRL: ...every club, pub and gig in the city.

CLUBBER: [*taking off trousers*] OK. You win. Here. Enjoy.

LOBB: [*grabs **Clubber** by the crotch*] I'd prefer you not to all me a twat sir. It would be more respectful to call me Nutter.

> ***Clubber** staggers away doubled up in pain, helped by **Girl**. Enter **Manager**. **Lobb** holds up trousers on one finger.*

LOBB: There you go, Adolf. That's a pony you owe me.

MANAGER: [*pays*] I'm not betting with you again, Nutter.

LOBB: That's a shame. Tomorrow night I fancied trying for a prosthetic limb.

> ***Manager** exits as **Lobb** steps forward, talking to audience.*

LOBB: I always feel better once I've squeezed someone's bollocks.

<u>Blackout.</u>

Other Plays by Peter Yates:

14 Seconds
Lie Detector
Truth Detector
Crazy Patterns
The Reality Checker
Urban Cycles [trilogy: *Dignity*, *Wages Day*, *Real Gone Kid*. Co-writer Jenny Wafer]
Big Yellow Taxi

www.randomcactus.co.uk

www.ingramcontent.com/pod-product-compliance
Ingram Content Group UK Ltd.
Pitfield, Milton Keynes, MK11 3LW, UK
UKHW041437180426
11947UKWH00007B/486